The Escape

Lynda La Plante is a Number One bestselling author. Born in Liverpool, she went to drama school and worked in theatre before becoming a television actress. She then turned to writing – and made her breakthrough with the hit TV series *Widows*. Her novels have all been bestsellers worldwide. Her script for *Prime Suspect* won many awards, and *Above Suspicion*, *The Red Dahlia* and *Deadly Intent* have been hugely successful for ITV in recent years. Lynda La Plante was awarded a CBE in the Queen's Birthday Honours List in 2008. She joined the Crime Thriller Writers' Hall of Fame in 2009.

Visit Lynda at her website:
www.lyndalaplante.com
Follow her on Twitter: @LaPlanteLynda

Also by Lynda La Plante

Quick Read 2012: The Little One

Wrongful Death
Backlash
Blood Line
Blind Fury
Silent Scream
Deadly Intent
Clean Cut
The Red Dahlia
Above Suspicion
The Legacy
The Talisman
Bella Mafia
Entwined
Cold Shoulder
Cold Blood
Cold Heart
Sleeping Cruelty
Royal Flush

Prime Suspect
Seekers
She's Out
The Governor
The Governor II
Trial and Retribution
Trial and Retribution II
Trial and Retribution III
Trial and Retribution IV
Trial and Retribution V

The Escape

Lynda La Plante

SIMON &
SCHUSTER

London · New York · Sydney · Toronto · New Delhi

A CBS COMPANY

First published in Great Britain by Simon & Schuster UK Ltd, 2014
A CBS COMPANY

3 5 7 9 10 8 6 4 2

Simon & Schuster UK Ltd
1st floor
222 Gray's Inn Road
London WC1X 8HB

www.simonandschuster.co.uk

Simon & Schuster Australia, Sydney
Simon & Schuster India, New Delhi

A CIP catalogue record for this book
is available from the British Library

Paperback ISBN: 978-1-47113-228-5
Ebook ISBN: 978-1-47113-229-2

Typeset by M Rules
Printed and bound by CPI Group (UK) Ltd, Croydon, CR0 4YY

MIX
Paper from
responsible sources
FSC
www.fsc.org   FSC® C014728

The Escape

During my research for the ITV series *The Governor* I worked with many prisoners and encouraged their writing projects. They told me many stories about their lives. *The Escape* is a work of fiction but based on a series of events told to me by two inmates. The names of the characters and the location of the prison have been changed. As that was some years ago, the prison systems have since been upgraded, but it remains a very moving and thrilling story.

Lynda La Plante

Chapter One

Colin lay on his prison bed, staring up at the ceiling. He had never in all his life felt as depressed and worthless as he did now. All he wanted was to be left alone in his one-man cell on West wing at Barfield Prison. His thoughts were cut into by the sound of the cell door being unlocked.

'Come along, Colin, you need to get your stuff together. It's time to move over to East wing and meet your new cellmate,' Officer Reardon said with a big smile as he entered the cell.

Colin rolled over and turned away from Officer Reardon, who sat down on the end of the bed.

'You can't let prison life get to you like this, Colin. I know you're deeply upset, but the Governor's not going to change his mind about your day release to be with Karen for the baby's birth. If you want someone to blame about being moved to another wing, then I can tell you that it was down to me.'

Colin, shocked by what he had just heard,

turned and looked at Officer Reardon. 'Why? Why do you have to move me? I'm not doing anything wrong and all I want is to be left alone. There's no crime in that, is there?'

'No, but I'm trying to help, not hinder, you, Colin. You haven't been eating properly or taking part in prison activities for nearly a month. You've shut yourself off and that's not good for your health, for your body or your mind. Having a cellmate will give you someone to talk to and help get you back on your feet again.'

Colin let out a big sigh. 'But I don't need anyone else to talk to, Mr Reardon.'

'OK, here's the deal. Give it a couple of weeks and see how it goes. Your new cellmate is called Barry. He's a nice young lad like you and he's looking forward to a bit of company. But, if it doesn't work out, I will get you moved back here. How's that sound?'

Colin still wasn't happy about moving, but he liked and respected Officer Reardon. In fact, not one of the inmates on West wing had a bad word to say about Mr Reardon. He was experienced and kind-hearted, and he often helped to make prison life bearable. Colin got up off the bed and started to remove the blanket and sheets to take with him.

'Good lad, Colin. I'll do that while you get your wash kit and other bits together.' Officer Reardon patted him on the back before starting to fold the blanket. Colin was ready to go after putting his few personal belongings in a clear plastic bag.

Colin Burrows was twenty-two years old and had two years to go before he had any chance of release on parole. He had pleaded guilty to burglary and handling stolen goods at the Crown court. The judge had granted him bail, but stupidly Colin went on the run. During the time it took police to find him, he had met and fallen in love with a beautiful and generous girl called Karen.

Karen had made him happier than he had been in his whole life. They got together when he found work as a painter and decorator for her father's small company, where she was a secretary. Because of Karen, and her family's support, he had been determined to go straight. They had been living together in Karen's two-bedroom flat in Croydon for a year when she agreed to marry him. A month after their small wedding, she had proudly told him she was pregnant. They were both thrilled, and had just set about decorating the box room as a nursery when the police came knocking at the door.

Colin's re-arrest had really shocked him. As the months had passed he had come to believe that the police had given up looking for him. Karen and her father had stood by him but they didn't know that Colin had previous convictions for petty theft. The judge took no notice of his having a job, his marriage to Karen or the fact she was pregnant. He was sentenced to a total of four years in prison.

Depression at the prison sentence had almost crushed Colin and he was shattered at being separated from Karen. He was relieved that she was still sticking by him and was visiting him regularly in prison. Her father had promised that, when Colin was released, he could return to work for him. But Colin doubted that would happen. His boss had been disgusted when he learned of his son-in-law's criminal record.

On her last visit Karen had said she would not be able to come again as the baby was almost due and she was finding it hard to travel. Colin broke down in tears when he got back to his cell and was so upset he couldn't eat. When his request to be released for the birth of his child was then denied, his depression grew worse.

Officer Reardon escorted Colin over to East wing, where they were met at the entrance gate by another officer. Officer Reardon shook Colin's hand and told him to cheer up, be positive and not to look so down in the dumps. Colin still felt very depressed, but he didn't want to upset Mr Reardon. He forced a smile and thanked him for his kindness. The other officer then escorted Colin up to his new cell, unlocked the door and virtually pushed him in. Then he slammed the door and locked it.

'Hi, I'm Barry Marsden, and you must be me new cellmate. Colin, isn't it?' said the man on the top bunk, sitting up straight with a big welcoming smile. 'I've only been in a couple of days. The officer said you're a first-timer like me and been in a few months, but you was a bit down so I should try and cheer you up.'

Barry Marsden was twenty-one, a jovial friendly young man on remand in custody from the magistrates' court. He was a bit overweight, and had a pleasant face, though he looked a little nerdy with thick jam-jar glasses and he had bad body odour.

A sad-looking Colin said nothing as he placed his belongings, wash bag, bed sheets and blankets on the bottom bunk. He sat down on the end of the bed, put his head in his hands and began to cry.

'Cor blimey, Colin, you is in a bit of a state. Fancy a game of "I spy with my little ..."?'

'No I don't. Just leave me alone,' Colin replied sharply.

Unlike most of the inmates, Barry actually liked prison life and more than anything enjoyed the three meals a day. He had come from a very difficult family, and had been in and out of a series of foster homes. Social Services had often been involved because of his step-father's drinking and violence. Barry's first attempts to make friends with Colin were met with moody silences, but finally his easy manner and persistence paid off. He felt very sorry for Colin, who was heartbroken that he would miss the birth of his first child.

Colin wrote endless letters and called home whenever he could, but hearing Karen's voice only made him feel worse. After a couple of weeks of watching his cellmate weep every night, Barry came up with an idea.

'I'm new to the wing, right? Nobody really

knows me, and I've never met any of the officers on the main gates.'

Colin shrugged, not at all interested, until Barry excitedly suggested the idea that he could, if they worked together, plan Colin's escape. Interested and slightly bemused, Colin asked what the plan was.

'It's simple. All we do is switch identities! You go in my place to the magistrates' court in a couple of weeks and do a runner when you get there,' Barry said.

At first, Colin thought it was the most stupid idea he had ever heard. Apart from having similar hair colour and being the same height, they didn't even look that much alike. And doing a runner from court was why Colin got four years in the first place. However, desperate to be at the birth of his baby, he decided to listen to more details of Barry's plan. The more the two of them discussed the escape, as far-fetched as the idea was, the more it seemed as if it might work.

Chapter Two

The two inmates whispered together through the night. Barry told Colin that it was usual to be questioned by the prison officers before being taken to court. As part of the plan, Barry told Colin everything about his life, explaining that it was important to remember as many details as possible. Colin listened intently as Barry spoke about his brothers, his mother and his violent step-father, who had given him regular beatings. Worse still was the abuse Barry had suffered at various foster homes. Colin worried about being able to keep all the facts straight in his head, because one mistake could cause the escape to blow up in their faces.

As Colin went on listening, he thought it was no wonder that Barry didn't want to leave the prison. After such a childhood, life inside was better. Barry said he was eager to further his education, and in prison he had the chance to do so.

He had begun art classes, and was showing great promise, so much so that he was allowed to keep a sketch-book, a variety of pencils and felt-tipped pens in his cell. Barry enjoyed copying pictures from magazines. He had never had such encouragement at home or school and, although he was a beginner, he was proud of his efforts. The prison art teacher had told him that, if he kept up his progress, he would be allowed to use acrylic paint and, in time, even oils.

The two cellmates became firm friends as they planned the switch, but time was running out. If the idea was to work, Colin had to feel certain he could take over Barry's identity. As part of the plan they made a point of never being seen together, and they always ate separately. Barry stayed in their cell as much as possible, and always kept his back to the door when the officers looked through the sliding hatch.

Colin went over Barry's life with him, again and again, so that he could answer any question Barry asked him about himself.

'OK, so where did I go to school?' Barry asked.

'St Thomas's.'

'How many GCSEs did I get?'

'None. You never sat any because you were expelled.'

Barry raised his hand. 'You're becoming a good me,' he said, as they slapped their palms together in a high five.

They were both growing confident that they could pull it off. Eventually, Colin could recall all of Barry's background, even down to aunts and uncles, addresses, dates of births and foster carers. They had left nothing out.

Colin was very careful not to mention anything to Karen when he spoke to her on the phone. She could sense that he was less depressed, and thought that he was now coping with their separation and prison life. She felt it was safe to tell him that she had asked the baby's sex at a recent scan, and that they were going to have a beautiful boy. Colin was overjoyed at the news and excitedly told Barry. They were now even more determined to make the escape plan work, so Colin could be with Karen at the birth of their son.

Colin knew he'd be arrested again, and that his escape would put his chance of parole in danger. He decided that, as soon as he had held his newborn son in his arms, and had kissed Karen, he would give himself up at the local police station.

'It'll only be a couple of days as her due date is the day of my escape. I'll convince the officers you had nothing to do with it. I'll say it was all my idea and I learned all about you from sharing a cell.'

Barry grinned and gave him a big hug. He had never had such a close friend. In fact, he'd not even been friendly with his brothers as they were much younger. He was thrilled and felt that, for once, he wasn't a Dumbo. Colin clearly liked him, and had been really appalled to hear about his abusive childhood. They agreed that, when both of them were finally released, they would stay friends. They even discussed working together painting and decorating.

'I doubt my father-in-law will take me back on, so we could set up our own business together,' Colin said.

'That would be brilliant. We could do up kids' rooms with, like, cartoon characters and stuff,' Barry replied with enthusiasm.

'Yeah, you draw them and then I paint them in. We could call our company BC designs.'

'I'm so excited, Colin. I've never had anything named after me before.'

Chapter Three

With two days and nights to go, Colin was feeling nervous and it was keeping him awake. They had still managed not to be seen together outside the cell, and they even went down to the showers at different times. The truth was Barry didn't shower that often, and his body odour was at times pungent and offensive. He even slept in his prison outfit, because, he said, he liked to be first in the line-up for breakfast.

It was early evening when their cell door was opened for shower time.

'I'll see you after your shower and we can go over everything again,' Barry said.

'I don't want to appear rude or anything, but I really think you could do with having a shower, Barry. It's been quite warm in here the last few days and ...'

'Sorry. I don't tend to notice it myself. You see, I don't really like taking showers, reminds me of school as I used to get teased and bullied about being a fat boy.'

'Well, we still don't want to be seen together outside of here so you go shower first.'

Barry nodded and picked up his towel. He was about to leave the cell when Colin stopped him and handed him a bar of soap.

Colin waited twenty minutes before going to the showers, as he suspected Barry would simply jump in and out again and he'd pass him on the stairwell. On entering the shower room, he noticed Barry stepping out of a cubicle and putting a towel round his waist. What Colin saw made him feel sick. Barry had tattoos over his chest, shoulders and right arm. Colin was so shaken he almost fainted. He'd never seen the tattoos before because Barry wore a long-sleeved denim shirt over his standard-issue cap-sleeved vest all the time. He got clean clothes only when he took one of his rare showers, which had always been after Colin.

By the time they had both returned to the cell, Colin was furious. Unable to control his anger, he grabbed Barry and pinned him up against the wall.

'You are covered in bloody tattoos!'

'I know. I had 'em done when I was drunk. Well, not all at once. Tattooist spelt some things wrong so I had to have some of them reworked. I got the mermaid and the ship when I went to Peckham and the . . .'

'Don't you understand?'

'Understand what?'

Colin wanted to slap him, he was so furious.

'They will ask me to take off my shirt and I haven't got a single bloody tattoo! They'll know I am not you straight away. It's finished. I can't get out now. You should have told me about your tattoos.'

Colin threw himself on his bottom bunk and buried his head in his pillow, sobbing. Barry felt dreadful. He had never liked undressing in front of anyone, and was always shy about his body. He had just presumed that Colin knew about the tattoos and was surprised that he had never seen them. He felt terrible, and after a couple of minutes went over and tapped his cellmate's shoulder.

'I know what we can do, it's possible we can get round the tats.'

Colin sat up and punched him away. 'How? How on earth can you think that? Walk out of here and visit a tattoo parlour, should I? Don't be so stupid. Just stay away from me, because right now I feel like punching your lights out!'

Barry looked totally dejected. At last, Colin

pulled himself together and calmly held out his hand. He gripped Barry's tightly. 'Sorry, I didn't mean what I said. It's my own fault. I just got so caught up in the thought of being with Karen again and seeing my son born. It was a dumb idea, and anyway I'd never have got away with it.'

'You still can,' Barry said excitedly.

'It's over, so let's just drop it. OK?'

'I've got a case full of felt-tipped pens and I can draw my tattoos on you. I could pat them down with your mouthwash to make them look older, more faded. I can do it, I know I can.'

Colin swung his legs down from his bunk and shook his head in despair at Barry's idea. He knew his cellmate was only trying to be helpful and, not wanting to upset him too much, Colin forced a smile.

'It won't work, and anyway that would make you an accomplice. Without the tattoo problem I could have said you had nothing to do with it. Even if you could draw anything like the ones you've got, it's too dangerous. They'll know you had to be in on it.'

'Now you just listen! I don't care if they charge me with helping you escape or add months on my sentence ...'

'But you're on remand and haven't even been given one yet, so you might just get released,' Colin said gloomily.

'I don't want to be released. I want to stay in prison, studying art and learning how to paint with oils. You are the best and only friend I have ever had, and I really want to do this for you. Besides, you are going to give yourself up after the birth, right?'

Colin nodded but was still uncertain. Barry sat beside him on the bed.

'We've come too far. You have worked so hard and learned every detail of my life and you have an amazing memory. You are really intelligent, you know that, right? Well, I'm not and I know that. It's not like you're breaking out to go robbing or assaulting anyone. You've got a good reason 'cos you want to hold your newborn baby boy in your arms. Give me a chance, Colin. Please, let's just see if I can make this work?'

Chapter Four

After a lot of discussion, Colin caved in, and decided that he should at least give the fake tattoos a try. He began to unbutton his shirt.

'Start on the right arm, as you'll never have the time to do my chest and shoulders. I could maybe get away with just rolling my sleeve up for the guards. Let's see how it looks first, before we decide to go ahead as planned.'

Barry grinned and went to his small cupboard and took out his case of felt-tipped pens. He began to select the pale blue, navy blue, green and dark brown.

'It'll be lights out soon, so I'd best get cracking.'

Colin took off his shirt and turned sideways for Barry to begin drawing on his arm.

'What I'll do is wet a tissue with mouthwash, and sort of press it against it to make it fade. I've had some of these tats since I was fourteen, so they're old.'

'Why did you get a ruddy mermaid?'

''Cos I'd never been to the seaside, and now I could say I had.'

Barry's ideas sometimes amazed Colin, but he said nothing as his cellmate concentrated and started to draw on his arm.

Colin kept getting up to check how it was going in the metal mirror above the small desk shelf. It was a very slow business as Barry wanted to make sure the tattoos were not only the right size but looked real. He knew the duty officers at the release desk would have details of inmates' tattoos to check against, as they had recorded all his when he first came in to Barfield. The mermaid was only half drawn when it was time for lights out. Colin had to admire Barry's work, and said it looked very realistic. Barry thought that the green was a bit too bright on her fish tail and would need to be faded down.

The next morning, Barry worked for an hour before bringing his breakfast of a bacon roll and coffee to the cell. Colin was so nervous he couldn't face eating and was worried that during the night the mermaid had become a little smudged. Barry went over the outline again, dabbed it with mouthwash and sprinkled talcum powder on it. His main worry was that he'd lost his yellow felt-tipped pen that he needed to draw her wavy blonde hair. He fiddled with the pens he did have, testing and mixing the different shades in layers on his notepad. In the end, the best match he could come up with was a watered-down orange.

Colin was getting more and more impatient as it was taking so long. Barry still had to do the outline and colouring of an anchor and chain on his shoulder, and they only had one day left to get it all completed. Colin tried his best not to put too much pressure on Barry, who sat concentrating very hard.

They both jumped when they heard the sudden sound of keys rattling in their cell door. Colin quickly pulled on his shirt and Barry pretended to be drawing in his art book as an officer unlocked the door.

'You two want to go down onto the wing floor to play in the table-tennis competition?' the officer asked.

'Thank you, sir, but we were about to have a game of chess,' Barry replied.

'Very brainy. I'll leave you to enjoy your game then,' he said, then turned and left the cell.

Colin breathed a sigh of relief. 'Just as well he didn't check.'

'Why?'

'We don't have a chess set, Barry, only dominoes!'

'Oh yeah, I forgot. You are really clever, and I just reckoned you'd know how to play chess.'

Chapter Five

After a couple of hours the drawings were taking shape and Colin grew more relaxed. They were making good progress and were both thrilled that nearly all the tattoos had been completed by lunch time.

'Only one more night to go,' Barry said as he checked his work on Colin's body, making some finishing touches. He felt much more confident now the job was nearly done, and started to pack away his felt-tipped pens before lunch. Meanwhile, Colin carefully buttoned up his prison-issue shirt over the freshly drawn tattoos. He was constantly afraid he would smudge them.

The cell door opened as an officer entered.

'Anything nice for lunch today, sir?' Colin asked, trying to appear calm.

'Well, there's prawn cocktail to start, followed by best fillet steak, mushrooms and fine-cut chips, with lemon tart for dessert,' the officer said with a cheeky grin.

'Sounds good to me, sir, will you be joining us?' Colin asked, playing along with the joke.

'I'd love to, but my wife would never forgive me for not eating her home-made ham, cheese and pickle sandwiches.'

'Well, I'd be happy to eat them for you and let you have my lunch,' Barry said, joining in with the banter.

'Believe me, the wife's sarnies aren't much better than what's served up in here,' the officer said, and they all laughed. 'Which one of you is Marsden?'

'I am, Sir,' Barry replied nervously.

'You're to report to the wing duty office right away.'

'What do they want?' Barry asked in alarm, and clenched his fists tightly to stop himself from shaking.

'You are leaving for court at eight tomorrow morning. They want to go over the details, so look sharp, son.'

'Yes, sir. Be right down, sir,' Barry murmured as he followed the officer out of the cell.

Colin was worried sick and couldn't face any lunch. Once again, he was becoming anxious and close to tears as he paced around the small cell, wondering when or if Barry would return.

Neither of them had expected a meeting the day before the court appearance. Colin was terrified that something might be wrong, and that they'd been found out. He calmed himself as he realised that they'd both have been summoned if the plan had been rumbled.

He sat on the edge of his bunk bed. 'Be positive,' he thought and he began to copy Barry's signature over and over again in his notebook. His friend had simple handwriting and, after only a little practice, he could almost do it with his eyes closed. Even so, in the pit of his stomach, he worried that everything they had planned and done so far might have been a waste of time.

It was nearly an hour before Barry came back to the cell. He was carrying a large clear plastic bag and, as the officer locked the door, he gave Colin a big smile and thumbs up.

'You won't believe our luck. I heard them saying that there are new officers coming onto the wing in the morning who won't have ever seen either of us.'

'What did they want with you?' Colin asked nervously.

'I, well, you pretending to be me, have got to be at the screws' office on the ground floor straight after breakfast. You need to put all my personal belongings in this plastic bag. I, I mean you, will then get escorted across to the release area, before being taken to Clapham Magistrates' Court.'

'This is madness, Barry. If I escape, I've then got to get all the way over to Croydon. We'll never get away with it.'

'Yes, we will. I heard them talking about a shortage of prison vehicles, and the senior officer said to use a taxi.'

'A taxi! Are you joking?'

'Nope, that's what I heard. Apparently, they regularly do it when they're short on paddy wagons and the prisoner is low risk like me.'

'Which officer is going to accompany you? Sorry, I mean me. What if he knows you?' Colin asked.

'I clocked the rota on the wall and it's an officer from another wing. Like I keep telling you, I've only been in here four weeks, so none of the screws knows me.'

'But he may recognise me and know I'm not you.'

'Not when you're wearing my glasses. The lenses are so thick even my mum would think you were me.'

'How on earth are you going to see then?'

'Don't worry, I got a spare pair.'

Colin was now really worried that they would never pull it off. But Barry insisted they had come so far that Colin couldn't back down now and miss seeing the birth of his son.

'So it's tomorrow then, eight a.m.?' Colin said nervously.

Barry nodded and clapped his hands, really enjoying the adventure. He had never been happier or felt so positive. Nor had he had such a close friend as Colin who depended on him so much. It all made him feel good about himself.

'We can do it, Col, but don't give anything away tonight when you talk to Karen on the phone. Take some deep breaths, keep calm and act normal.'

Chapter Six

They were lying on their beds, waiting to be let out for dinner, and had not spoken for a while. Colin broke the silence and asked Barry if he ever made phone calls home.

'No, not got a phone card and there's no one who'd listen anyway. Nobody gives a toss about me. They never did.'

'I do. I care a lot about you, and I won't ever forget what you're doing for me. I owe you big time.'

Barry beamed. It felt great to have a friend like Colin. It was a deed well worth doing, just to know that he could help him be present at the birth of his son.

As usual during dinner, they ignored each other and ate at separate tables. The change-over officers had just begun their shift and would be on duty for the night. The next shift would take over before breakfast, at 6 a.m. the next morning.

*

After dinner, Colin joined the telephone queue to call Karen. She was very down, saying that she was so heavily pregnant she could hardly move.

'The last scan was good, and everything's on schedule for the birth tomorrow. Mum's going to take me to the hospital. She's even packed a bag for me.'

'I love you so much and you'll be fine,' Colin said, desperately wanting to tell her he would, if all went to plan, be with her.

'I wish you were going to be with me, Colin. I miss you so much and I really need to see you. It's been weeks and I don't know how I'll be after the baby is born. I hope I'll be able to travel to the prison. My mum has bought a VW for me to use so that will help. I know I'll be able to bring the baby with me at visiting times, but it's just not having you here to give me support, and I get really scared.'

'You keep strong, darling. I will be thinking of you and our baby every minute of the day.'

'I know, but it don't help, because I miss you so much.'

Colin was getting upset as she started to cry. He changed the subject, trying to distract her by asking if she'd thought of any other names to call their son. They often talked about this, and she had said that her favourite name was Justin, after the pop singer Justin Bieber. Colin said that he had been thinking about what name he would like the baby to be called.

'Why? You'd agreed to him being called Justin.'

'I know, but can we call him Barry instead and maybe have Justin as a middle name?'

'Barry!' Karen exclaimed.

'Yeah, do you like the name?'

'No, I don't. What do you want to call him Barry for?'

'Listen, darling, next time I see you I will explain it all.'

The prisoner behind him tapped on Colin's shoulder, and pointed to his watch. Time was up on his call. Not wanting a row, Colin said goodnight to Karen and hung up. He had so wanted to tell her that he would soon be with her, but had managed to stop himself. He couldn't help being really happy, as he was starting to feel more and more certain that he could pull it off. Until now, he had been doubtful, but hearing her voice made him very excited. He was nervous, yet he firmly believed that in only a few hours he would be with Karen.

Chapter Seven

When Colin returned to his cell, Barry was looking at a comic on his bunk bed.

'Guess what we decided to call him?' Colin asked with a big smile.

'You'd told me Karen wanted to call him Justin.'

'I changed her mind. We want him to be called Barry.'

Barry sat up, his eyes brimming with tears.

'You mean that? You would do that?'

'Yeah, if that's all right with you?'

'Of course it is. Wow! That's the nicest thing anyone has ever done for me. I really appreciate it, Colin. Thank you so very, very much.'

'That's OK. Let's just hope it all goes to plan in the morning.'

The lights went out, and they both lay on their bunks as the cells were locked up for the night. There were the usual catcalls and tinny radio sounds that would continue into the wee hours. Neither of them had a radio. They had talked about maybe getting one, but they had no money and no one brought one in for them. They had sometimes watched television in the communal TV room, but deliberately never together, so if one saw a show he would tell the other all about it.

'Do you want a final run-through?' Barry whispered.

Colin whispered back that it would be a good idea. Quietly, they went through all of Barry's relatives, his childhood and school days until they had covered everything. At last, they fell silent.

'Not long now,' Barry said after a while.

'Fingers crossed,' Colin answered, yawning.

After a few minutes, he could tell that Barry had fallen asleep because he snored, but Colin just couldn't get to sleep himself. He was too wired, thinking about what it would be like to see Karen and how she would react. He thought about her parents, and worried that her father might tell the prison or police where he was. He decided that he would explain to Karen's mum and dad that he had been let out on day release for the baby's birth.

If everything was on time and the baby was born on the due date, he was certain he would get away with it. They had planned that Barry would stay in the cell all morning and not go down for his lunch or mix with the other men on the wing. He prayed that Barry, who would have to pretend to be him, gave nothing away before he himself got to court and carried out the final part of his escape. He also hoped that he would have plenty of time before the prison officers started asking Barry questions and found out the truth.

Unable to sleep, Colin paced round the cell. He looked over at Barry, sleeping like a baby apart from the snoring. He sincerely hoped that his friend would not get into deep trouble for helping him. Colin had considered tying Barry up and gagging him, but quickly realised that was a stupid idea which could give away everything at an early stage. He had even suggested that Barry should say that he was threatened and forced to do the tattoos and swap places, but Barry had rejected the idea. He would rather just play dumb and act as if he had forgotten about the arrangements for his court appearance. He also told Colin that he did not mind getting months added to his sentence, as he preferred prison life to his life outside.

Colin had tried to make him aware of what it could mean, as Barry had not even been convicted of a crime yet, but was on remand until the magistrates' court sent him for trial. It was during that conversation that Colin learned exactly why Barry was at Barfield.

'I was charged and kept in custody for stealing food.'

'Stealing food! What was it, an Iceland truck full of the stuff?' Colin had asked, astonished.

Barry laughed. 'No, McDonalds and KFC.'

'Burgers and chicken?'

'Along with French fries and a large drink. I'd even order a triple Mac with double fries and the warmed apple pie. I was doing it like every day, sometimes twice, and always ran off without paying.'

Colin shook his head in disbelief as Barry continued, 'I waited until all the food was on the tray and then, when they asked me for the money, I'd pick it up and run like hell.'

'Didn't you spill it off the tray?'

'The first few times, yes, and I was only left with the chips or burger. The more I did it, the better I got and eventually never spilled a thing. One time though the drink went all over the floor, and the manager who was chasing me slipped in it and went arse over tit!'

They both laughed out loud as Barry recounted his balancing skills.

Colin was surprised that Barry's crime, which seemed little more than a minor theft, was serious enough for him to land up in prison on remand. Barry giggled and explained that he had been dodging paying for his fast food for as long as he could remember.

'I've been arrested loads of times, given warnings, fines and probation.'

'Then why haven't you learned your lesson?'

'Because I just can't resist doing it. I know every fast-food place from Chelsea to Fulham, Putney to New Malden, Kingston and beyond. You name an outlet and I'll have tapped 'em.'

'You must be a walking satnav for fast-food joints,' Colin said.

'I'd always return the tray,' he said with a shrug. 'I'd leave it in their doorway after eating the food. I had to keep switching where I went, so that the staff wouldn't recognise me. I never thought I'd get caught, but they got me in Clapham High Street last time.'

Colin was taken aback as it was a ridiculous series of petty crimes that didn't, in his opinion, warrant a prison sentence.

'Why are you going for trial and pleading not guilty? If you plead guilty at the magistrates' you might not even get a prison sentence.'

Barry giggled again. 'Because I know that I will be found guilty and get a longer sentence at Crown court. You see, Colin, I'm glad they got me. I don't really want to go anywhere else. I'm even going to ask for two hundred other cases to be taken into consideration.'

Colin could not understand Barry's attitude. He himself hated being in prison and had always thought that Barry was just making the best of a bad job when he'd claimed otherwise. Now he realised that Barry was genuine, and that Barfield was the closest thing he had to a family and home.

Colin still felt extremely bitter that after going straight he'd been locked up for crimes he had committed over a year before. He was angry that the judge had not taken into consideration that he had changed while he was on the run and had been hard-working and honest. It had meant nothing to the judge that he had married Karen, she was pregnant and they were due to start a family together. It hadn't helped that when Colin had been caught he had put up quite a struggle. Although all he had done was to push the arresting officer over, the judge described him as 'violent' and, peering at Colin over his half-moon glasses, had spoken in a clipped cold manner.

'You were originally due for a sentence of probation and community service. You alone chose to abscond, and the courts will not tolerate that type of behaviour. You only have yourself to blame. Justice will be served and you, young man, are going to pay your debt to society.'

Chapter Eight

Colin went back to bed, but he tossed and turned and kept checking the time. The night seemed to go on forever, and he was growing more and more restless. He decided that, when he did give himself up, he'd start to use his time in prison more wisely, especially since he wanted to win back his chance of early parole. He would apply for the educational programmes and really try to better himself.

The more he thought of it, the more certain he became that, after the baby was born, his life would improve. He knew that in his teenage years he had been very rebellious and often, as the judge had said, he could be quite violent and had got into scraps. But after meeting Karen, he had calmed down. Now he hoped, when he gave himself up after the escape, he would be sent back to Barfield Prison and would share a cell with Barry again. They could study together and he would take classes in computer studies and business, or anything that would give him a greater chance of work when he was finally released.

At some point, he must have dozed off, because suddenly Barry was shaking him awake. It was 6 a.m. and they needed to double-check that none of the tattoos had smudged. Satisfied they were still intact and looking very realistic, they switched clothes. Barry was a lot plumper than his friend and the shirt looked too large on Colin, but he tucked it loosely into his prison-issue jeans to make himself look bigger than he was. Barry put on Colin's shirt and started to button it up. It was very tight so he decided it was best to let it hang open, exposing the white prison vest.

He looked at Colin and shrugged his shoulders. 'I've lost a bit of weight since I was arrested. It's not eating all the takeaway food. You'll have to tighten up my trousers. They look too big on you and the last thing you want is them falling down.'

Barry chuckled as Colin hitched up the jeans.

Eventually, their cell lock clanged as an officer opened the door at breakfast time. Colin grabbed Barry's glasses from his face as the officer entered and checked his clipboard.

'Which one of you is Marsden?' the officer asked, and Barry, by force of habit, was about to answer, when quick-thinking Colin jumped in.

'Me, sir.'

'Go have your breakfast and then make your way to the wing staff office. An officer will escort you to the release area for processing before going to court.'

'Yes, sir, I know, they explained it all to me last night,' Colin said, as his heart thumped rapidly.

The officer was new and didn't even give them a second glance as he moved on to the next cell.

Barry and Colin both breathed a sigh of relief.

'I nearly dropped us in it there, but so far so good,' Barry whispered.

'Yeah, and I'm not even out of the cell yet,' Colin said, wiping his brow.

'He hardly even looked at us, and I've never seen him before,' Barry said confidently.

'Right, you go and get your breakfast and I'll wait until eight to go to the wing.'

'Slight problem there. If I'm supposed to be you now, I can't really wear my glasses, and I can't see a bloody thing without them,' Barry said.

'Oh no, I didn't think about that,' Colin replied. He was starting to sweat with nerves. He waved his arms to cool himself. He was worried that if he sweated too much, it might make the tattoo ink run. 'Just wear your spare pair if you have to. Like you said, the officers are new so hopefully no one will notice.'

'Right you are, good luck, and I hope all goes well with the birth,' Barry said. He was sad now that it was nearly time for Colin to go.

Colin had never been very touchy-feely, but he put his arms around Barry and patted his back while he hugged him.

'Thanks for everything, pal.'

Barry gave his friend a big grin and put his thumbs up. 'Ta-ra for now.'

Chapter Nine

Left alone, Colin sat on the edge of his bunk. He'd been nervous when he woke up, and now his body was shaking and he was finding it hard to control. He took deep breaths, and listened to the noise of the inmates making their way to the canteen. He almost fainted when someone rapped on the cell door and an officer looked in on him.

'Not going down for breakfast?'

'No, sir. Got a bit of a dickey tummy from the shepherd's pie last night.'

'Oh, right,' the officer said and went off down the corridor.

Colin took more deep breaths to try to calm his nerves. He watched the minutes tick by very slowly until ten minutes to eight. Then he collected Barry's things, his art pad, his crayons and felt-tipped pens. He put them in the plastic bag along with Barry's wash bag, which held his toothbrush, razor, shaving cream and comb. By the time Colin had stripped Barry's bed and folded the sheets and blanket, it was two minutes to eight and time to go.

He paused by the cell door and took the art pad, crayons and pens from the bag and hid them under Barry's pillow. Colin knew how important they were to his friend, and he reckoned he could do without them.

With the bag and the bedding stacked in his arms, his head was only just visible above the pillow. He could hardly see a thing as the thick lenses of the glasses blurred everything. He pushed the glasses to the end of his nose so he could peer over the top of them, and walked out into the empty corridor, moving slowly. He walked down the iron staircase and on towards the wing's staff office. There was only one officer on duty. He was eating a bacon sandwich as Colin appeared at the open door. Colin gave Barry's name and number and waited, his heart pounding hard inside his chest.

The officer popped his last bite of sandwich into his mouth, checked on a notice board and then looked at his wristwatch. He put in a radio call for another officer to come to escort prisoner Marsden to the release area for processing. Colin hoped that his shaking legs would not give the game away.

'You had breakfast?' the officer asked.

'Yes, sir,' Colin lied, not wanting to speak any more than was necessary.

He remained standing as the officer drank his coffee and read the newspaper. It was ten minutes before there was a call to say the escort was at the wing entrance. The officer, irritated by the interruption, tossed the paper aside, picked up some paperwork and gestured for Colin to follow him.

They had to walk the length of the recreational area of the wing, then along a narrow corridor to the barred gate, where a female officer was waiting. Colin was relieved as he had never seen her before. The male officer handed her the paperwork, saying it was prisoner Marsden's court release file.

Colin was amazed that she didn't even check the file before unlocking the gate and stepping to one side to let Colin pass in front of her. The officers chatted for a while and it was another few minutes before the gate was relocked. She then gestured for him to walk ahead of her along the corridor. It seemed to go on and on forever, until finally they reached another gate.

At each gate, CCTV cameras were filming them and the female officer would come to a stop, show her key, and speak into a microphone.

'Officer Stoodley taking Prisoner 8724 Barry Marsden to reception gates for court appearance release,' she said every time in a bored voice.

Once that was confirmed, the gates opened electronically and the officer used her key to open the last lock. Each time, Colin stood with the stack of Barry's things in his arms, his heart jumping in his chest. They turned down what seemed like endless corridors, crossed the exercise area and eventually reached the entrance to the prisoners' main reception area.

Colin frantically wondered why they were there. He was relieved, when the gate opened, to discover that the reception was also used for release.

There was a long counter, where several officers were taking details from inmates. Some were being released, others were also on their way to various courts, and, on the opposite side, were new arrivals.

'All right, Barry, love, you go over there and wait to be called.'

'Yes, ma'am,' Colin said as he shuffled across to sit on a bench beside two other inmates holding their stuff on their knees. He didn't look up and just stared at the ground, terrified someone would recognise him. The thick glasses blurred everything, and he hoped he wouldn't fall over when he was called.

Colin waited for what seemed to be an extremely long time. The incoming inmates were quite noisy and shouting abuse. The officers were dealing mainly with them rather than the men waiting to be released or to go to court. Colin watched as the new inmates were given prison-issue clothes and wash bags, and told to go into the changing rooms. Once they had changed into prison uniform, their personal items were bagged, tagged and put in lockers.

Eventually, the man sitting next to him was called to the counter. Colin watched as he was told to put down everything to be checked. They then brought out his personal items in a bag that contained street clothes and smaller objects, a wallet and mobile phone, which he had to sign for. Colin didn't want to appear too interested, in case it gave him away, but he listened intently as the officer double-checked the man's belongings. He then began asking him questions about his address and his family, and Colin shuddered when he saw the officer compare the prisoner's face with a photograph on his file.

'Shit,' he said to himself. Did he look enough like Barry even with the jam-jar glasses on? Could they be mistaken for each other? No way: they were of the same height and even had similar hair colour, but Barry was fatter and they didn't look that much alike. He was so shaken that he didn't hear the name Marsden. It was only when the officer called 'Marsden' a second time that he took any notice.

Colin jumped up, stepped forward to the counter and set down the blanket, towel and pillow. The officer calmly threw them into a large laundry skip before opening his wash bag and sifting through it. A sealed plastic bag containing the clothes Barry had worn on his arrival was brought out. Inside were also a wallet and a key ring, which were placed on the counter with the clothes. The officer turned the personal items form towards Colin for signing and handed him a pen. For an instant, Colin thought about how many times he had practised writing Barry's signature. His palm felt clammy, but he knew he could get it right. He signed Barry's name.

The officer told him to go to a changing cubicle and put on his own clothes for the court appearance. Colin took off the prison-issue jeans and shirt and stood in his underpants and vest as he pulled on a terrible moth-eaten, stained pair of navy-blue jogging pants. They were much too large for him and he hitched them high up around his chest. Dirty white trainers and socks all smelt horrible. He was just reaching for the T-shirt when the curtain swished to one side and an officer peered in.

'I need to inspect your tattoos.'

The man looked at his clipboard, which had a piece of paper with an outline of a man printed on it and a list giving the type and position of Barry's tattoos.

'Keep calm, keep calm,' Colin repeated to himself in his mind as the officer glanced at his arm and then looked more closely at the mermaid before he pulled the curtain closed. Colin breathed a sigh of relief, swallowed hard and reached over to pick up the well-worn T-shirt. It had a faded logo of a Coke can on it. He tried to ignore the foul smell as he put it over his head and then pulled it down to cover the top of the jogging pants. He folded the prison clothes into a neat pile and then carried them back to the counter. The tattoo check was over and his confidence was growing that Barry's insane plan would actually work.

Chapter Ten

Colin handed the prison clothes to an officer and they were also tossed into the laundry bin. He was told to sit on the bench again and wait. Within a few minutes, another officer picked up Barry's release file from the pile on the counter.

'Prisoner 8274 Marsden, step forward.'

Colin went to the counter, where he was asked for his address, his family's address and where he was born. While he was able to answer with ease, he was now tense because the officer was ticking off his questions and turning the page to Barry's prison photograph. Colin was filled with fear. Even though he'd got away with the tattoo check and being questioned about Barry's family, he had not thought this would happen.

In the next instant, all of his plans for escape could end in disaster, and any hope he had of seeing his newborn child be ruined. All he could do was pray that Barry's glasses would be enough to fool them.

'You look as if you've lost weight. We've got you down here as fifteen stone.'

'Yes, sir, I was charged with nickin' food from McDonalds. That was all I ever ate, so since I've been here, I've lost a few pounds.'

The officer laughed, and was about to look at the photograph, when all hell broke loose. One of the new prisoners had thrown a punch and was screaming and shouting. The distraction was enough to make the officer tell Colin to take his release documents and wait in the holding area.

'Get a move on. You've got a taxi waiting and an officer will take you to court.'

The fight grew worse and no one paid any attention as a relieved Colin grabbed the release documents and walked out into the holding area. He was dying of thirst but had to wait in line. The inmate ahead of him was handing over his documents and being released, having served his sentence. The electric metal door opened and the ex-prisoner began to sing at the top of his voice as he danced across the yard towards the next and final exit to the outside world.

Colin hoped he would be as lucky. He handed over his file and a muscular, grizzled and grey-haired senior officer briefly checked the forms. He stamped a piece of paper, handed it to Colin and dropped the rest of the file into a plastic tray marked COURT RELEASES.

'You got a taxi and an escort officer waiting in the yard by the exit gate,' he said.

'Thank you, sir.'

Colin stepped forward, but the big man put out his arm.

'Not so fast, son, just let me make sure they're ready for you.'

He spoke into a radio microphone, announcing Marsden was ready to go and would be the next prisoner to exit.

Colin had the release form, Barry's wallet and key ring in one hand and was holding up the loose jogging pants with the other. A blast of cold air took his breath away as the gate opened. He gingerly stepped into the courtyard and his spirits rose when he saw the massive set of wooden gates. Another female officer was standing by a local taxi firm's rather beaten-up Volvo and an officer with an Alsatian on a lead was checking the car over. Colin handed her the release form.

'I've been waiting for you, and at this rate we are going to be late for your hearing at

Clapham,' she said as she opened the rear door of the taxi. Colin went to get in, but she stepped in front of him and got some handcuffs out of a pouch on her belt.

'Hold your hands out please.'

Colin felt dejected as he hadn't expected to be handcuffed. It wasn't as if Barry was some big-time dangerous criminal. He was just a small-time thief who liked to nick fast food. Colin put out his hands for cuffing and could now only hope that they would be removed when he got to court. He got into the back of the Volvo and the female officer sat beside him. She was a pleasant-looking blonde, in her late thirties. The officer with the dog opened the main gate and the taxi drove out.

Colin couldn't believe he'd got this far, as the officer turned to speak to him.

'This is my second trip to the courts this morning, so I had the chance to speak with your solicitor. You're on remand, aren't you?'

'Yes, ma'am, I'm going to be committed for trial today.'

'Well, your solicitor wants you to change your plea to guilty this morning. Because you've been at Barfield for a month, there's a good chance it will count as time served and you'll be released from custody at court. He also said the magistrate will give you credit for the other offences you've admitted.'

'That's good,' Colin said happily, realising that he now had a way of walking out of court legally rather than having to escape by doing a runner. His excitement was short-lived though, as it dawned on him that the solicitor was another problem he and Barry had overlooked. Barry had never even mentioned him, let alone described him. He'd only told Colin that his solicitor had suggested that he should be medically assessed for his fast-food obsession and his learning difficulties, which were due to lack of schooling. These could be used to get a lesser sentence.

Colin knew Barry was not the brightest spark and had noticed that he struggled with reading. He seemed only ever to look at comics, saying that he liked the pictures. Colin also knew that if Barry appeared before the magistrate, he'd never change his plea to guilty. He desperately wanted a trial and to be found guilty so he could stay in prison. Colin thought it was harsh for someone like Barry to be locked up with tough criminals for such a petty crime as stealing food, and really he should have been sent to a hospital for treatment instead.

'You're very quiet, Marsden,' the officer said, giving him an encouraging smile.

'Yeah, lot of things on my mind,' he replied and then asked how long before they got to court.

'Be about another fifteen minutes.'

However, it took a lot longer as they got stuck in a traffic jam because of road works. It wasn't Colin who began to get agitated but the prison officer. She kept on looking at her watch, shaking her head and moaning about the hold-up. They were crawling along and she was worried that, if he missed his time slot in court, they might have to delay the hearing and that would ruin her whole timetable.

'I'm getting worried. Maybe I should contact your solicitor?'

That was the last thing Colin wanted. The solicitor might ask to speak to him and that could give the game away.

'Don't they turn off their mobiles when they are in court, ma'am?'

She sighed and looked at her watch again.

'I don't know what to do. You see, I've only just completed my training and I've been working at Barfield for just six weeks. I used to work in a dry cleaner's, but I'm a single parent so I really needed a better wage packet.'

Colin said nothing as the car inched forward and eventually started to pick up speed as the traffic thinned out. It was a further ten minutes before they drove into the parking area of the court.

Chapter Eleven

The prison officer opened the car door for Colin and walked with him to the entrance. They went into the court along a stone corridor and headed into the prisoner reception, where she took off the handcuffs. She should have taken Colin down to the cell area, but instead told him to sit and wait while she asked if his case had been called yet. She became even more anxious when told that his solicitor was already in court with another client.

Colin sat watching and listening, wondering when, and if, he could find the moment to escape. The officer was pacing up and down, unsure what to do, when the door to the court opened. The defendant in the previous case was led towards the cells and the female officer went through the door to try to get the solicitor's attention. Colin looked round. No one was taking any notice of him and he knew it was now or never. He stood up and calmly headed back down the corridor to the door through which they had entered.

Colin walked slowly across the rear car park and out of the open gates, and then ran as fast as his legs would carry him up the street. He had to keep a tight hold of his baggy jogging pants as they kept slipping down. Nervous and confused, he asked a couple of passers-by the way to the nearest bus station because he knew the Underground did not go as far out as Croydon. The depot was half a mile down the road. On the way, Colin nipped down a side alley and turned Barry's T-shirt with the Coke can logo inside out. Arriving at the bus station, he looked in Barry's wallet, to find nothing, not a penny. He knew that by now the prison officer would have realised he'd gone and had probably told the police. He looked round in despair and saw a man get off his bike at a newsagent's shop and rest it against the wall. He didn't want to take it, but felt he had no choice.

Karen meanwhile was at home checking her hospital bag with her mother. She was feeling scared as they had been told that she should not contact the hospital unless her waters broke or she had regular contractions. She wasn't sure, but she had begun to feel twinges in her belly. Her mother kept on asking if she was all right and, at the same time, checking they had the due date written correctly on the calendar.

'I just want to have the baby!' Karen wailed.

'I know you do, love, but they'll only send you back home if you're not really ready. Often, it's a few days either side of the due date. When your waters break you'll know ... and right now, they haven't, have they?'

'I want to be there early to make sure they have a bed for me.'

'Of course they'll have a bed for you on the maternity ward. Just sit down for now and try and relax. I'll make us a nice cup of tea.'

Karen slumped onto the sofa, near to tears. She felt like a beached whale, and her emotions were in a mess.

'I wish Colin was here,' she said tearfully.

'Well, you've known for some time that he can't be. The prison refused him permission to be with you, but I'm here. I won't leave you, so just relax. You're all packed and ready, and I can drive you there when the time is right.'

Karen suddenly let out a yelp of pain and held onto her stomach.

'It's time, Mum. I can feel it. We've got to go NOW!'

By now there was complete panic at Clapham Magistrates' Court. At first, it was assumed Colin had gone to the toilet, but after a search of the building it was obvious that he had simply walked out. The prison was contacted and the local police arrived at the court as the poor newly trained prison officer broke down in tears.

She explained about the traffic jam, that they were late for court, and how she had been trying to find out when Barry Marsden's hearing was going to happen. By now, his solicitor had joined them and said that, had Barry appeared and pleaded guilty, it was more than likely he would have been released that morning. He joked that they would probably be able to find him in the nearest McDonald's, and, if not there, they should try KFC.

As Barry Marsden was not a high-risk category 'A' prisoner, there was little concern for public safety. He had never been known to be aggressive or violent, so the police inspector didn't feel the need for an urgent public appeal. This took a bit of pressure off the situation. However, his escape certainly made the prison and court officers appear totally incompetent, which in itself was a serious matter.

The prison authorities would be furious, and the police would have to begin a search even though they felt it was the prison's fault. The police immediately gave Barry Marsden's description to all local patrol officers. They also sent all his personal details to the police stations near his family, so that officers could visit his relatives and find him as quickly as possible.

Of course, the police were searching for the wrong person, as the prisoners had swapped identities. This gave Colin added time to make his way home. He dumped the bike away from his flat. He was exhausted from all the frantic pedalling on the eight-mile journey. He rang the doorbell and waited for someone to answer. When no one did, he realised Karen must have gone to hospital or be at her mother's. He needed to change before he could do anything else and remembered that they kept a spare key with their neighbour.

The neighbour was an elderly lady who was hard of hearing and took a long time to answer his desperate ringing of her doorbell. Eventually, she opened the door and was very surprised to see Colin. He asked for the spare key, and said as little as possible so as not to alarm her or give the game away.

'I'm allowed home to be with Karen for the baby's birth,' he said, impatient for her to give him the key to their flat.

'Oh, how nice. She left about an hour ago with her mother, who said they were off to the hospital.'

'Had she started labour?' he asked as she handed him the key.

'Not sure, but she was clutching her tummy and moaning a lot.'

Colin thanked her for the key and hurried off to his flat. Once inside, he ran into the bedroom, threw off Barry's smelly clothes and scrubbed off the tattoos with white spirit. Wanting to look good for Karen, he then had a shower, washed his hair and shaved. Having put on a clean shirt and jeans, Colin searched the flat for some money so he could get a taxi to Croydon hospital. He thought the first thing the police would check would be buses and the Underground.

Karen's waters broke as she arrived at the hospital, and she was helped into a wheelchair by one of the porters. Her mother was beside her, holding her daughter's hand tenderly as they were taken up to the maternity ward. Her mother unpacked the nightdress and baby bag, and Karen sat on the edge of the bed as another contraction began. She moaned, holding onto her belly, and her mother rubbed her back to try to comfort her. A nurse gave Karen a hospital gown to change into, and then a midwife examined her pelvis to find out what stage of labour she was at. She also checked the baby's heart rate.

'Will the baby's father be joining you for the birth?' the nurse asked politely.

'I wish he was, but he's away on business,' Karen replied between deep breaths.

Chapter Twelve

The police arrived at Barry Marsden's home address on a run-down estate in Peckham, South London, but no one was there. They also called on two relatives who appeared not to care and said they had not seen him in years. As the solicitor had suggested, they also began to check the fast-food joints near the court-house and his local shopping centre, but without success.

One hour later, Colin arrived at the hospital and at once spoke to the receptionist. Checking Karen's name on the computer, she asked who he was. Colin, fearing the prison or police might call the hospital, said he was her brother. She told him that Karen was in the maternity ward on the third floor. He pressed for the lift but, when it didn't come immediately, he was so impatient that he ran up the three flights of stairs. Excited and out of breath, he took a while to explain to a nurse that he was Karen's husband and he'd rushed over from his work. The nurse checked her clipboard and smiled.

'You are in luck, Mr Burrows. She's in labour but the baby's not arrived yet. She's just been taken to the delivery room.'

The nurse took Colin to the delivery wing, where she spoke to a rather plump senior nurse who handed him a gown and mask.

'She will be pleased to see you. Your wife is quite a feisty young lady and she's getting impatient, but she's not dilated enough yet. It shouldn't be long though. Try and help calm her down.'

Colin's heart was pounding as he was led towards the delivery room. Suddenly he heard a woman screaming and he knew it was Karen. He stopped for a minute to take a few deep breaths, and then walked through the double doors.

Karen was wearing a soft protective bath hat over her long blonde hair and a hospital gown. He could hardly see anything except her feet, which were in stirrups, and the bulge of her tummy. Her mother was sitting sweating beside her, and Karen was gripping her hand so tightly she was half out of the chair. At first, her mother didn't recognise Colin because he had the mask on, but then she let out a shriek, shouting out his name.

'Colin! It's Colin. He's here, Karen.'

Karen tried to raise her head, but let out another scream and flopped back as she was having such a painful contraction.

Colin took her mother's chair and leaned in close, taking her hand.

'Karen, it's me, my darling. I'm here for you and our baby.'

She was screaming and panting hard, and yet so pleased to see him that she started to cry.

'They released me so I could be with you,' he lied, and bent in to kiss her forehead.

'Come on, Karen, give a good push now. We're nearly there.' The doctor came forward and Karen's face twisted with pain.

'Deep breaths now, Karen, and one more big push,' he said firmly.

She gave one last groan, a big heave and the next minute the baby boy arrived. The midwife quickly weighed and washed him, and then handed him to Karen, wrapped in a white sheet. Karen was by now propping herself up, holding out her arms, and Colin broke down in tears. They both wept, because it was such a wonderful moment. Their baby son was perfect in every way and they were overwhelmed with joy.

Colin had never felt such happiness and

love. When Karen carefully passed the baby for him to hold in his arms, he thought his heart would burst with pride.

'My God, Karen, he's beautiful. He's even got hair and look at his tiny fingers.'

As Karen's mother watched them together, any bad feelings she had about her son-in-law vanished. Colin's joy and tenderness were touching. His obvious love for Karen made her mother realise that they were a beautiful couple who deserved to be together. No matter what she thought about Colin being in prison, seeing him with her daughter and grandson meant that he was family. Her husband might not be quite so easily won over, but she'd talk to him at home.

Karen was wheeled back into the maternity ward. She was feeling very tired, but having Colin beside her made all the difference. She was so happy. Delighted with the healthy baby boy who was placed in a crib beside her bed, she smiled at her loving husband as he sat in the chair next to her.

'I am so glad they agreed to let you be with me,' she said, holding onto his hand.

'Me, too, I wouldn't have missed it for the world.'

'I love you, Colin.'

'I love you, too, and Barry.'

She wrinkled her nose and asked if he still really wanted to call the baby Barry.

'Maybe, a bit later, I'll explain why, but please agree. Like I suggested before, his second name can be Justin.'

Colin stayed with Karen all afternoon. She slept for a couple of hours, and her mother went home. Her father arrived with a bouquet of flowers. He was not very friendly to Colin but, after seeing him proudly cradle his grandson, he too changed his mind. He said that he was glad that the prison authorities had allowed him out for the blessed event. He asked how long he would be able to stay with Karen before he had to return to Barfield.

Colin said that he had to go back after forty-eight hours, not even hinting that he had escaped. Although he had intended to tell Karen, there never seemed to be the right moment and he didn't want to upset her. There would be time later to confess to her that he had actually absconded.

Chapter Thirteen

The search for Barry Marsden went on, but the police still had no idea where he was. They returned to his home address and this time his mother was in. She had been shocked to hear that he had escaped from the court, and claimed to have no clue as to what he was up to or where he could be. When the police searched the house, she became vicious, outraged that they doubted her word.

'Believe me, if Barry had turned up here, I would have reported him immediately. He's never done anything but cause me trouble,' she said bitterly.

'Sorry, we're just doing our jobs, ma'am,' a fresh-faced policeman replied as they went on searching the house.

As his mother had insisted, he wasn't there, but, as the police were leaving, they asked for a list of anyone she thought he might be in contact with.

'None of the family, I can tell you that for

66

certain. He's just a ruddy loser,' she said with a coldness that sounded cruel.

Eventually, she gave the police some names and numbers, but told them it was a waste of their time. The police thanked her, but felt no further forward than when they had started.

Barry's other relatives and known contacts were also questioned, but no one had seen or heard from him, and no one seemed to care a jot about him. The prison authorities were not happy. They didn't care that Marsden was a low-risk prisoner. The fact was, he had escaped and that made them look bad in the public eye. When the police reported back that they were unable to trace Barry, the Governor of the prison ordered the cell to be searched for any clues. He also said that Barry's cellmate, Colin Burrows, was to be brought to his office for questioning.

By late afternoon, East wing was buzzing with rumour and speculation among the inmates. A prisoner returning from a different court had heard two officers in reception talking about a prisoner who had escaped. The officers were trying to lay the blame squarely on the female officer who'd escorted Barry Marsden.

'What, the wimpy guy with the jam-jar glasses?' a fellow inmate asked.

'Yep, so don't expect the screws to be in a good mood tonight.'

Barry was lying on Colin's bed reading a comic when the officers unlocked and flung open the cell door. Then they dragged him into the corridor so they could carry out a search. He'd managed to take off his glasses and hide them in his hand without being seen.

'Governor wants a chat about your cellmate, Barry Marsden. Seems he's disappeared. You know anything about that, do you?' one officer asked, and poked him in the chest.

'No, sir. He's at court, sir.'

Barry kept his head down and tried to slip his glasses into his pocket. The officer, wondering what he was trying to hide, grabbed his hand and twisted it hard. Barry yelped in pain and dropped the glasses. That was the moment the game was up, as the officer pulled his head back by the hair and recognised him as Barry Marsden, the presumed missing prisoner. At the same time, they found the art pad and felt tips that Colin had hidden under Barry's pillow.

*

The other prisoners on the block, who were watching through their cell-door windows, shouted, swore and banged loudly on the doors. They were outraged at the way a helpless fellow prisoner was being treated. Barry picked up his glasses, put them back on and moved slowly along the landing. The officer got impatient and grabbed hold of him, forcing him to walk faster. Some of the prisoners recognised Barry now he had his glasses on, and knew that it must have been Colin Burrows who had escaped. There was more jeering and swearing at the officers. It was part shock and part admiration of an inmate who had so daringly escaped using the identity of his cell-mate.

Barry was really scared as he was manhandled and dragged through the corridors to the Governor's office. He was shaking uncontrollably as he stood to attention in front of the Governor's desk with a prison officer either side of him. At first, he still tried to pretend to be Colin, but one of the officers gave him a hard clip round the back of the head. He then claimed that prisoner Burrows had never told him anything about an escape plan. The Governor, who was now seething with anger, got up from his desk and went nose to nose with Barry.

'I'm not a fool, so don't make it any worse for yourself, son. Just admit that you helped him with his escape plan because YOU had to know about your court appearance, right?'

'I might have been told, sir, but I just forgot about it.'

'Well, you'd better start remembering quickly, or you'll be in solitary confinement for months, without so much as a piece of chalk to draw with!' the Governor shouted, and again an officer slapped the back of Barry's head hard.

He was really frightened now, and couldn't face the thought of being in solitary with no art book, felt tips or pencils. Sobbing and terrified, he changed his story and admitted that he had known about the plan. He said he was scared of Colin Burrows and had to agree to let him take his place for the court appearance.

'Did Burrows threaten you?'

'Yes, sir. I was afraid not to do exactly what he told me.'

'Do you know where he was planning to go?'

'All I know is that he was desperate to be with his wife. She's having a baby, sir, and he said he would do anything to be there at the birth.'

70

'Did he say which hospital?'

'No, sir.'

'Take him back to his cell,' the Governor snapped angrily.

He was worried that the press would get hold of the story, and that he and his staff would be made to look like a bunch of incompetent fools. He also knew that it could mean the end of his career in charge of Barfield Prison.

As Barry was dragged back to his cell, he got a huge cheer when the inmates saw him. They all started singing as loud as they could, 'There's only one Barry Marsden', repeating the words over and over. The officers felt they were being made to look like idiots and, in anger, threw Barry back into his cell. He hit the floor and wall really hard, hurting his right shoulder and arm. He wasn't sure if he'd broken it, but he didn't dare say anything as he knew the officers wouldn't care anyway.

'You are going to get a lot of extra time inside for this. Believe me, we'll be watching your every move from now on.'

The cell door slammed shut as Barry crawled onto Colin's bottom bunk and curled up in pain. The cell was a mess after the search. The officers had broken all his felt tips into pieces and thrown them in the toilet.

The fact was many of the prison officers were going to be investigated for having allowed the escape to occur. The male officers had all been smug at first, trying to blame it on the female officer who'd escorted Colin on the court run. They now realised they were all in big trouble, and there were plenty of excuses as the officers argued and accused each other. Prisoner Burrows had fooled everyone who had dealt with him that morning. If just one of them had done his job properly and checked more closely, they would have recognised the switch and prevented the escape. Now some of them might even lose their jobs.

Chapter Fourteen

The police couldn't believe it when they were told that the escaped prisoner was actually Colin Burrows. The prison sent his picture, a full description and his home address with a plea that they find and arrest him as soon as possible. They also told them that his wife Karen was pregnant and due to give birth, so they should check local maternity wards in case Burrows was there.

Colin's freedom was to be short-lived. Police forced entry into his flat and, finding nothing, spoke to the elderly neighbour. She was quick to reveal she'd seen Colin and he had gone to hospital to be with his wife. At the same time, other officers went to Karen's parents' address, hammering on the front door. Her mother, frightened out of her wits, opened up. She was certain something terrible had happened, and screamed as they pushed past her, shouting that they were looking for Colin Burrows.

'He's at St Mary's hospital,' she sobbed.

They radioed back this information, but paid

her no attention as they searched her house. She insisted that her daughter had just given birth, and that Colin had permission to be there.

'No, he hadn't. He's an escaped prisoner.'

'Oh, my God! Oh, my God, my poor daughter! This is awful.'

Sirens blaring and blue lights flashing, two patrol cars, with three officers in each, pulled up in the hospital car park and ran into the building. It was terrible. The nurse on duty was told to keep calm and point out which bed Mrs Burrows was in and if her husband was with her. They made the nurse so nervous that she was gasping for breath, but from the double-doors opening onto the wing, she was able to show them Karen's bed. The man they wanted was sitting beside his wife, cradling his new-born son in his arms.

Colin couldn't help but hear the rumpus and, seeing the uniformed police in the doorway and the panic-stricken nurse, he knew his time was up.

He stood, looked them in the eye and turned to Karen.

'I'm sorry, darling, I lied to you. I never had permission to be here. I pretended to be someone else, and did a runner from prison so I could be with you. It looks like the cops are here for me.'

Three of the uniformed officers entered the ward, trying not to alarm all the new and expectant mothers. One officer called out for everyone to remain calm.

'Come on out now, Burrows. Don't scare everyone. Just walk towards us slowly and keep your hands up so we can see them.'

Colin kissed his son on the forehead before handing him to Karen, who was in floods of tears. He leaned forward to kiss her as well, but she turned her head away. He felt totally dejected and rejected as he held his hands up and began to walk between the rows of beds. The noise had woken most of the sleeping babies and they were howling.

As Colin reached the officers, they snatched him and turned him roughly, pressing his face against the wall as they handcuffed his hands tightly behind his back. The cuffs hurt as they pinched his skin. The officers grabbed him under the arms and dragged him forward, slamming his body against the swing doors as they headed for the lifts. They pressed for the lift, but it was on the top floor so they pushed him towards the stairs.

'There's no need to be so rough. I'm not causing you any trouble.'

Colin half turned, wanting to explain he was giving himself up quietly and that he had only escaped to be at the birth of his son. Suddenly he lost his footing and, with his hands cuffed behind him, couldn't regain his balance or grab the safety rail. He fell down an entire flight of the staircase, hitting his head hard against the wall. The officers ran down to help him onto his feet. He had a big round red mark on the side of his head, which was already starting to swell up, and his nose was bleeding.

By the time they got him to the patrol car, blood had dripped down his shirt. The driver got out and quickly opened the rear door.

'What happened to him?'

'Tried to do another runner and tripped down the stairs. Banged his nose, but it's his own bloody fault,' one officer said and threw Colin onto the back seat.

The patrol car screamed off with its blue light flashing. An officer radioed in to report that they had recaptured Colin Burrows and were taking him back to Barfield Prison.

The prison gates opened as the patrol car was signalled to enter. Four prison officers were waiting as the car stopped. Colin was dragged out, his head throbbing and the swollen red mark turning into a bruise. He felt dizzy and sick to his stomach. The police officers handed him over to the prison guards, explaining that the bruises and bloody nose were down to him trying to avoid arrest and escape again. One policeman even laughed and said, 'They don't run or get away from us once we nick 'em.'

The prison officers didn't think it was funny, but Colin was so angry he stepped forward and kicked out, calling the policemen liars.

It was the worst thing he could have done, because his move made it look as if he had become violent. One of the prison guards punched him hard in the chest, knocking him backwards to the floor. The next second, he was turned over with his face to the ground while the police handcuffs were taken off and replaced with a prison set. The police left as the guards pulled Colin up hard by his arms, which felt as if they were being jerked out of their sockets. They then pushed him through the gate into reception.

The officer who had given him final clearance that morning was waiting angrily as they dragged him in. He was in a foul mood, because he had been called before the

Governor to explain exactly how he had allowed Colin to escape, and had been given a severe roasting. He knew he might be sacked or forced into early retirement, and he was furious. He walked over to Colin and took hold of his face in his big lumpy hands and squeezed tightly.

'You are going to be very sorry, Burrows. Your life in here won't be worth living when we're done with you.'

Colin was in a great deal of pain and made yet another big mistake, one he would regret for the rest of his life. Unable to use his hands, he brought his knee up and kicked with all his might into the officer's crotch. The guard let out a howl of pain. The two officers behind Colin swept his legs from beneath him, so that he crashed yet again face forward onto the concrete floor. He tried to get up, but one of them used a baton to hit him over the head. He wasn't sure how many times he was hit as the blows were so painful and hard that he passed out.

Chapter Fifteen

Colin woke up the next morning in the hospital wing. His bandaged head was throbbing and his left hand was cuffed to the iron bed post. His mouth felt dry, and he had a horrible bitter taste in his mouth from the dried blood. His face was aching terribly and he had lost two teeth.

The prison doctor examined him a few hours later. Colin was feeling dreadful. His head still throbbed and his jaw ached. In fact, his whole body felt like lead. The doctor unbuttoned Colin's shirt but said nothing as he looked at the awful bruises. He felt his ribs, then his stomach, pressing it with his fingers and causing Colin to flinch in pain. He shone a torch into Colin's eyes and ears, then asked him to open his mouth. Clicking off the torch, he picked up the clipboard from the end of the bed and made notes. Colin moaned with the pain.

'Well, that's what happens when you run off

and accidentally fall down stairs, Mr Burrows,' the doctor said without sympathy.

Colin tried to answer him, but he was in such agony that he couldn't find the energy. He wanted to explain just how he got the injuries, but the words would not come out. They felt trapped inside his mouth.

'Just stay calm. You'll remain here for a while, and I'll check on you again tomorrow.'

A week later, Colin was still in the hospital wing, but the handcuffs had been removed. The bruises were healing and turning banana yellow. He still had headaches, but, thankfully, they had not been too bad, and he slept for most of the time during his recovery.

The Governor had visited him on his second day in the hospital wing. The interview had been short and disturbing. As soon as Colin's condition improved, he was to be placed in a high-security wing with loss of privileges for two months and solitary confinement. He was told he was very lucky that his sentence had not been extended but, if any other incidents arose, he would be given more time inside. Colin knew that the truth was the Governor was embarrassed by the whole affair and just wanted it to be forgotten as soon as possible.

Taking more action, such as holding a hearing to increase Colin's sentence, would just drag it out.

Colin learned that Barry Marsden claimed that he had been threatened into aiding the escape. The Governor believed that, because the man had learning difficulties, it had been easy for Colin to force him to help with the plan. Colin wanted to defend himself, to say that it had been Barry's idea in the first place and that he had in no way threatened him, but he said nothing.

The Governor was aware that Colin had been injured during his arrest, but warned him that it would not be wise to make a complaint. If he chose to ignore the Governor's warning and did complain, the rest of his time at Barfield would be very uncomfortable.

'Do you have anything you wish to say?'

The Governor waited for him to reply. Colin still said nothing. It was partly that he didn't want to get Barry, or himself, into further trouble. But it was also because he was finding it difficult to form the words. It was as if his brain was not working properly. He knew what he wanted to say, but he just could not get the words out.

'I know, Burrows, that you wanted to be with

81

your wife for the birth of your child. I also know that permission was refused and that you simply decided to ignore the ruling and escape. But rules are there to be obeyed, not broken. You are serving a prison sentence for your crimes. You must now face the punishment of remaining here for your entire sentence without any hope of an early release.'

So that was it, and there was nothing Colin could do about it. He closed his eyes, not wanting to show that he was close to tears, as the Governor turned and walked off with a smile on his face.

Colin stayed in the hospital wing until his injuries were healed and the doctor said he could return to the main prison. They had given him painkillers and were concerned that he was again suffering from depression. The doctor suggested that he be watched with regular visits to his cell. Colin had not spoken to anyone the entire time he had been in the hospital wing, and had answered queries only with grunts and nods. They assumed he was just being difficult and that he still had anger issues.

Colin was deeply angry. He felt that no one understood. He had never been allowed to explain what it meant to be refused permission to be at the hospital for his child's birth. He had never even been able to say that he had always intended to return to the prison.

It felt as if the world was against him, and worse still was having no contact with Karen. He had no phone card as he had left it with Barry when he had escaped. He had no money to buy another one, and he wasn't sure they'd allow him to make calls even if he did have one. Besides, he wasn't certain he would be able to speak to her, as he had not been able to form a single word since his so-called 'accident'. It seemed that all he could do was grunt, and he was getting more and more frustrated. He thought about writing a note to the doctor, but decided not to bother as he thought that, after his escape, the man would just ignore it.

The strain was getting worse and he felt that the only thing that could make him better would be seeing Karen. Only she understood him, and only she could help pull him out of this awful mess and depression. He just hoped that he hadn't upset her too much. He wanted so badly to talk to her face to face, to explain himself, and hoped that she would forgive his stupid mistake.

*

Karen had been shocked when Colin had been arrested at the hospital.

How could he have put them both in that kind of danger? Her mother and father were equally disgusted, and they didn't accept the apology that Colin had given Karen as he was taken away. He had lied to them, he had lied to Karen, and they knew he had ruined any hope of an early parole. Karen was also depressed, since she was finding it difficult to cope with the new baby and she couldn't sleep from worry. She needed her mother's help and decided to move back in with her parents.

Soon, the small flat she and Colin had rented was taken over by another young couple. Karen had moved all her possessions over to her parents' house and the couple bought what little furniture was left.

Karen wrote to Colin only once, and her father read the letter before she sent it. He suggested that it would be best for Karen and the baby to make no visits and to have no further contact with Colin. Also, it must be clear that there was no longer a job open to him on his release.

Chapter Sixteen

Colin received Karen's letter on his first day back on the new wing. He shared a cell with a tough illiterate prisoner, serving eight years for armed robbery and grievous bodily harm.

Barry Marsden appeared at the magistrates' Court four weeks after Colin's escape. He was persuaded by his solicitor to plead guilty. His months on remand counted as time served against his sentence and he was released from prison. The magistrate arranged for Barry to be placed on a twelve-week care-in-the-community programme, where he would be monitored, but could go on studying and having therapy. Once he got out, Barry had applied for visiting rights to see Colin, but had been turned down.

Eleven months passed before he was given permission to visit Colin. Barry now wore contact lenses, had lost a lot of weight and was dressed in a smart suit. He looked healthy and felt good. Thanks to Social Services and various charities that found work for ex-offenders, he was an apprentice plumber. He sat in the waiting room at Barfield, looking forward to seeing his friend, scanning the faces of the inmates as they were let into the visiting section.

He was not the only one whose looks had changed. Barry was shocked to see how poorly Colin looked. His dark hair was greasy, his face gaunt and unshaven, and he had a hollow look in his eyes. He seemed to shuffle rather than walk, and his prison-issue denims looked filthy and crumpled. At first, Colin didn't recognise his friend without his glasses. Then, when Colin sat down opposite him, Barry noticed how Colin sort of crouched and darted frightened glances around the room.

'I have been trying to come and see you for months,' Barry said.

Colin did not reply and Barry patted his suit lapel. 'I got a job and bought this so I'd look respectable. I'm working as a trainee plumber and I really love it. I'll work with a qualified bloke when I finish my training.'

Colin still said nothing, and Barry began to feel nervous.

'I wanted to come and say that I never meant to make out that you threatened me. They slapped me about and sort of put words into my mouth. Truth was, when everyone got to hear about the escape, it give me a lot of respect. I'd never been so popular. Everyone wanted to be my friend.'

Colin still stayed silent, and Barry was finding the one-sided conversation difficult. He blurted out that he had passed his driving test.

'On the second attempt. I failed the first one 'cos I didn't indicate I was turning left and I got a couple of the road-safety questions wrong. Where can you park on a motorway was one. I said that I could park on the hard shoulder, but that's wrong. You are not allowed to park anywhere on motorways. Did you know that?'

Colin stayed mute.

'What I should have said was, in an emergency you can stay on the hard shoulder to call for help. It was a trick question.'

As Barry looked at Colin, he noticed beads of sweat running down his forehead. It was awful, and he couldn't understand why Colin wouldn't talk to him. He was certain that his friend blamed him for his arrest and capture, but he had only been trying to help.

'Listen, Colin, I'd do anything for you. I'd even swap places with you again, if it would help.'

The bell to signal the visiting time was over was going to ring at any moment. Barry was almost in tears, and then, slowly, Colin reached over to grip his hand.

'No ... ooo ... No ... not your fau ... fault.' It was hard to understand what he was saying as his speech was so slow.

'Why you talkin' funny?' Barry asked.

'I can ...'t s ... top sllurr ... ing ... sin ... ce ... I hh ... hit my ... my he ... ad ... when I fell.'

'Bloody hell!' Barry exclaimed, and held onto Colin's hand. 'Have you seen Karen and the baby?'

Colin shook his head, and Barry leaned in closer to whisper.

'Did the officers do this to you?'

Colin nodded, with tears in his eyes.

'Does Karen know what happened, or the state you're in?'

Colin shook his head and tried to explain, but he stammered so badly that it took a long time for him to say that he had no money to buy a phone card to make calls. Barry knew that he couldn't write a letter about being assaulted because the prison officers checked letters. If they saw anything like that, they would destroy it.

As Barry sat listening, Colin's stammer got worse as he became more upset. Barry was sorry to hear that Karen had not been to see him and that she and the baby had moved out of their flat and in with her parents.

'You can write though, beg her to come and see you and then explain everything. Promise me you'll write to her?' Barry said, looking directly into Colin's eyes.

The bell rang. Neither man was ready to say goodbye, but the officers told the prisoners to go back to their cells, and there was nothing they could do. Colin gave Barry a weak smile as he joined the line-up of inmates, and then a small wave of his hand before wiping his tears on his shirt cuff.

Barry sat for a while, feeling wretched and sad. Colin had been such a bright spark, really intelligent and, more than anything, a man with a dream of his future. He was determined to go straight and had been so excited about becoming a dad. He adored his young wife and should have his whole life ahead of him, but now he seemed broken. Barry felt awful because he had encouraged the escape, and now it had destroyed Colin's hopes.

Barry went to the exit, where he recognised the officer who was standing by the doors. He knew he shouldn't, but he was so upset about Colin that he stopped and glared at him.

'You bastards, what you done to Colin? He can't even talk right any more.'

The officer hardly recognised Barry, but then stepped back a fraction.

'Don't you go pointing the finger at any of us. He did a runner, made everyone look like idiots. He fell. No one touched or pushed him. He fell, all right? And, if you really are his mate, then you give him some advice. Tell him to behave himself. Tell him to stop fighting the system, and to go and have some sessions with the therapist for anger control. Because, if he goes on the way he's going, he'll be banged up for a few more years.'

Barry walked out and into the visitors' car park, where he had left his ten-year-old red Ford Escort. It had a lot of mileage on the clock, but he owned it. He sat inside it, watching all the visitors leaving in their various vehicles – wives and kids, brothers and sisters, mothers and fathers – and it made him feel deeply for his friend. Colin had no one. He had not seen Karen or his son since the child's birth, and that was about a year ago.

Chapter Seventeen

Later that day, Barry was still so distressed that he almost walked out of McDonalds without paying for his hamburger and chips. He caught himself and delved into his pocket for the right money, before taking his tray to a table to eat his meal. By the time he had finished, he knew what he was going to do and he was going to do it now.

Barry hoped that he had the right address. He remembered Colin talking about his father-in-law's decorating business, which was near his home. He got help at the library from an assistant to look through the Yellow Pages for the address of Scott's Decorators. Then they used the register of voters and found the home address in a nearby street.

It was early evening, and it had taken Barry a good two hours to drive there. The small end-of-terrace house was spotless. The garden was well cared for, with potted plants in large urns by the sage-green front door. It all looked freshly painted and well maintained, as befitting the house of a builder and decorator.

He rang the doorbell, and waited. He was nervous, and kept on patting his tie and fiddling with his collar to make it sit flat. The door opened and suddenly Karen was facing him. He recognised her from the photographs he had seen in the cell he'd shared with Colin.

'Hello, Karen,' he said quietly, realising that she was even prettier in real life.

She looked at him, puzzled, wondering who he was. 'Yes, can I help you?' she asked.

'I'm Barry, a friend of your husband's.'

Before she could say anything, there was a wild yell. Crawling towards her shapely legs at an astonishing pace, Barry saw a blue-eyed toddler. Now a year old with a head full of dark hair, he was the spitting image of Colin, and he chuckled with joy as Karen bent down to scoop him up in her arms.

'Justin, you be a good boy.'

At that moment, an elderly man came up the small garden path and stood directly behind Barry.

'Who's this?' he asked sharply.

'Hi, Dad. He says he's a friend of Colin's, but I don't know him.'

Next, Karen's mother came to the door to ask what was happening.

'He's another convict like that no-good husband of hers, and he's not welcome in my house,' Karen's father said, wagging his finger at Barry.

'Please, Mr Scott, I'm just asking for a few minutes of your time,' Barry pleaded.

'We don't want anything to do with Colin or anyone connected to him. You can clear off and tell him my daughter is going to divorce him,' he said, and started to close the door.

Karen's mother stepped forward and held the door open. 'We should at least listen to what this young man has to say.'

Her husband turned his back and started to walk away, but his wife was firm. 'And that includes you as well, my dear!'

They all sat in the nicely furnished lounge, which had a floral carpet, velvet sofa and matching chairs. Barry had never in his life had to deal with a task like he was now facing. He knew he would have to keep calm and speak steadily, as he could sense Karen's parents' mistrust and hostility after he had told them who he was. Karen held the little boy on her lap as he cuddled a soft teddy bear.

Barry took a deep breath and, as nervous as he was, he knew it was very important that he explain everything properly.

'Colin wanted more than anything to be with Karen at the birth. He was heartbroken when the prison wouldn't let him, and he became very depressed.'

'Well, he only made things worse by trying to escape,' Mr Scott said.

'That wasn't Colin's idea. It was mine. He didn't want to do it, but I persuaded him it would work and then he and Karen could be together,' Barry said.

Mr Scott let out a huffing sound. 'And once the baby was born? What was he going to do then ... go on the run again?'

'Honestly, he was going to give himself up. He didn't want to cause any trouble for any of you. He just wanted to be with Karen at the birth.'

They sat in silence as Barry broke down in tears. 'He's in a bad way and very depressed. If you saw him, you wouldn't believe the state he's in.'

'What do you mean? Is he sick?' Karen asked.

'I think he was badly beaten by the prison officers, but I don't know the full story as he can't speak properly and slurs his words.'

'I don't understand. Is that because of the beating?'

Barry nodded before continuing. 'He didn't escape to do any crimes or hurt no one. He just wanted to be at the hospital for you. You've got to go visit him and let him see and hold his baby boy. It's only right.'

Karen hugged her little boy close and started crying. Her mother had to go and fetch a box of tissues, as she had started crying, too. Only her father was still surly and unforgiving, as he refused to believe a word of what Barry had told them.

'You've got to visit him, Karen. I will drive you there and back whenever you want to see him,' Barry said.

'No grandson of mine is going to be taken to a bloody prison. Having my daughter married to that man is bad enough.'

Barry stood up, facing Karen's father.

'That's not fair. You know that he was straight during the time he was working for you. He was doing good and got his life on track. Are you saying that doesn't count for anything? Didn't he work hard for you? Didn't he love your daughter? Won't you at least help a man who risked everything to be with Karen when she gave birth? Your son-in-law is not a bad bloke, but you leave him inside with no hope and he will turn bad.'

Karen's father was still not convinced and his wife asked to speak to him alone in the kitchen while she made a pot of tea.

'Are you blind?' his wife asked.

'What do you mean by that?'

'Can't you tell how much Karen misses Colin? Deep down she still loves him so, when we go back in there, you will support her decision, whatever it is. Do I make myself clear?'

Her husband paused. 'Yes, if that's what you want,' he finally agreed.

They went back into the living room, carrying the tea and a tray of biscuits.

'Do you want to see him?' Karen's father asked, though it was still clear that he disapproved.

Karen looked at her mother. She had always found it difficult to stand up to her father, even more so lately, as she and the baby were living under his roof. Her mother nodded and Karen turned to her father.

'I want to see him, Dad. I don't know if we'll ever get back together, but I need to see him and at least talk to him. Colin has the right to see Justin and, as he's just a baby, he won't even know he's in a prison.'

*

It was agreed and that, whenever Karen was ready to visit, Barry would drive her there. Barry was able to drive home feeling that he had finally done the right thing. His own life had changed greatly since the escape and, unlike Colin's, it was entirely for the better. Now he hoped that his dear friend's life would change for the better as well.

Chapter Eighteen

The visit from Barry had made Colin face the truth. He was destroying himself, drowning in self-pity and letting the system win. He decided to do whatever he could to improve his life. He signed on for anger-management therapy. Perhaps with expert help, he could control his stammer, and find a better way to deal with all of his unruly feelings. He was also accepted onto a writing course, which gave him a chance to express himself and something new to think about.

Colin's stammer didn't go away, but he found that nothing halted the flow of words when he wrote things down. Writing helped him communicate and feel better about himself. His rehabilitation was not immediate, but what drastically raised his spirits was the news that Karen was going to come and visit him.

Barry was as good as his word. When Karen wanted a visit, he collected her and waited in the car park for her to come out again. He never asked to see his old friend then, because he felt they needed the time to be together as a family. He visited on his own, and as often as he could.

After a few visits, Karen brought Justin, who could now stand and totter along, to meet his dad.

Colin was sitting, waiting expectantly. When he saw Karen heading towards him, and holding his son's tiny hand, he felt an incredible joy.

'This is your daddy,' she said as they drew close.

Colin opened his arms and the little boy was unsure for a moment, and then said 'Dada', before holding out his arms, too. Colin realised Karen must have shown Justin pictures and explained who his father was. He picked him up and held him close and loved the silky feel of his thick curly hair and the smell of his baby skin as the boy said 'Dada' over and over.

Karen continued to come back. She loved watching Colin with Justin, but their visits were always charged with sadness. It seemed that as soon as she relaxed and felt comfortable with Colin, the visiting time was up and she had to leave.

They did not discuss divorce, and she did not

seriously think about it. She still loved Colin and she wanted to help him get better so that they could have a life together. To add to her hopes, her father had at last accepted her decision and was now writing to the authorities to say that he would have a job waiting for Colin on his release.

Colin was very different now, much calmer and quieter than he had been before.

Writing had proved to be an incredible means of healing for him, and he began to study with great enthusiasm. He often gave Karen a list of books he wanted to read and she happily brought stacks of them in during her visits. Over time, he grew more confident in his ability and even planned to study journalism.

Karen treasured the letters she got from him, each one thoughtful and filled with his love for her and Justin. His writing gave her a greater insight into the person he really was, a tender man who had known hardship, but whose desire now was only to make amends.

Colin's description of seeing his son born was touching and very beautiful. Karen kept that letter closest to her heart. She planned to read it out in church at their son's christening, but she was waiting until Colin was released so they could celebrate that blessed event together, as a family.

She now knew why Colin had wanted to call their son Barry. They didn't argue, but agreed with all their hearts that Barry would be his second name, and Barry himself would be Justin's godfather.

Justin Barry Burrows would never know the details of his father's outrageous escape or the painful aftermath that had changed the course of his life. By the time Colin was released from prison, his speech was nearly back to normal, he had won three writing awards and was beginning a career as a trainee journalist with a local paper. What Justin did know was that he had a loving and happy family, and a kind-hearted Uncle Barry who drew great fake tattoos.

Books In The Series

Amy's Diary	Maureen Lee
Beyond the Bounty	Tony Parsons
Bloody Valentine	James Patterson
Blackout	Emily Barr
Chickenfeed	Minette Walters
Cleanskin	Val McDermid
The Cleverness of Ladies	Alexander McCall Smith
Clouded Vision	Linwood Barclay
A Cool Head	Ian Rankin
A Cruel Fate	Lindsey Davis
The Dare	John Boyne
Doctor Who: Code of the Krillitanes	Justin Richards
Doctor Who: Made of Steel	Terrance Dicks
Doctor Who: Magic of the Angels	Jacqueline Rayner
Doctor Who: Revenge of the Judoon	Terrance Dicks
Doctor Who: The Silurian Gift	Mike Tucker
Doctor Who: The Sontaran Games	Jacqueline Rayner
A Dreadful Murder	Minette Walters
A Dream Come True	Maureen Lee
The Escape	Lynda La Plante
Follow Me	Sheila O'Flanagan
Four Warned	Jeffrey Archer
Full House	Maeve Binchy
Get the Life You Really Want	James Caan
The Grey Man	Andy McNab
Hello Mum	Bernardine Evaristo
Hidden	Barbara Taylor Bradford

Lose yourself
in a good
book with Galaxy®

Curled up on the sofa,
Sunday morning in pyjamas,
just before bed,
in the bath or
on the way to work?

Wherever, whenever,
you can escape
with a good book!

So go on...
indulge yourself with
a good read and the
smooth taste of
Galaxy® chocolate.

Proudly supports

Read more at **f** Galaxy Chocolate

Quick Reads are brilliant short new books written by bestselling writers to help people discover the joys of reading for pleasure.

Find out more at **www.quickreads.org.uk**

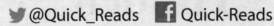 @Quick_Reads 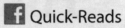 Quick-Reads

We would like to thank all our funders:

LOTTERY FUNDED

We would also like to thank all our partners in the Quick Reads project for their help and support: NIACE, unionlearn, National Book Tokens, The Reading Agency, National Literacy Trust, Welsh Books Council, The Big Plus Scotland, DELNI, NALA

At Quick Reads, World Book Day and World Book Night we want to encourage everyone in the UK and Ireland to read more and discover the joy of books.

World Book Day is on 6 March 2014
Find out more at **www.worldbookday.com**

World Book Night is on 23 April 2014
Find out more at **www.worldbooknight.org**

Start a new chapter

Hidden

Barbara Taylor Bradford

Drama, heartbreak and new beginnings.
This is a gripping story from a master storyteller.

On the surface, Claire Saunders has it all. She has a rewarding
career in fashion and a talented concert pianist daughter. Her
loving husband is one of the country's most trusted diplomats.

But every now and again, she has to plaster her face in heavy
make-up and wears sunglasses. She thinks she's hidden her
secret from her best friends, but they know her too well.

Can her friends get her out of harm's way and protect
her from a man who is as ruthless as he is charming and
powerful? And along the way, can Claire learn to stop
protecting the wrong people?

Harper

Start a new chapter

Blackout

Emily Barr

You wake up in a strange room,
with no idea how you got there.

You are abroad, in a city you have never visited before.

You have no money, no passport, no phone.

And there is no sign of your baby.

What do you do?

Headline Review

Rules for Dating a Romantic Hero

Harriet Evans

Do you believe in happy endings?

Laura Foster used to be a hopeless romantic. She was obsessed with meeting her own Prince Charming until she grew up and realised real life doesn't work like that.

Then she met Nick. A romantic hero straight from a fairytale, with a grand country estate and a family tree to match.

They've been together four years now and Laura can't imagine ever loving anyone the way she loves Nick.

Now, though, Nick is keeping secrets from Laura. She's starting to feel she might not be 'good enough' for his family.

Can an ordinary girl like Laura make it work with one of the most eligible men in the country?

Harper

Start a new chapter

Four Warned

Jeffrey Archer

These four short stories from a master storyteller
are packed full of twists and turns.

In Stuck on You, Jeremy steals the perfect ring for his fiancée.

Albert celebrates his 100th birthday, and is pleased
to be sent The Queen's Birthday Telegram.
Why hasn't his wife received hers?

In Russia, businessman Richard plots to murder his wife.
He thinks he's found the answer when his hotel
warns him: Don't Drink the Water.

Terrified for her life, Diana will do whatever it takes to stick to
the warning given to drivers: Never Stop on the Motorway …

Every reader will have their favourite story – some will make
you laugh, others will bring you to tears. And every
one of them will keep you spellbound.

Pan Books

Start a new chapter

A Cruel Fate

Lindsey Davis

As long as war exists, this story will matter.

Martin Watts, a bookseller, is captured by the king's men.
Jane Afton's brother Nat is taken too. They both
suffer horrible treatment as prisoners-of-war.

In Oxford Castle jailer William Smith tortures, beats, starves
and deprives his helpless victims. Can Jane rescue her sick
brother before he dies of neglect? Will Martin dare to escape?

Based on real events in the English Civil War,
Lindsey Davis retells the grim tale of Captain Smith's
abuse of power in Oxford prison – where many
died in misery though a lucky few survived.

Hodder and Stoughton

Why not start a reading group?

If you have enjoyed this book, why not share your next Quick Read with friends, colleagues, or neighbours.

A reading group is a great way to get the most out of a book and is easy to arrange. All you need is a group of people, a place to meet and a date and time that works for everyone.

Use the first meeting to decide which book to read first and how the group will operate. Conversation doesn't have to stick rigidly to the book. Here are some suggested themes for discussions:

- How important was the plot?
- What messages are in the book?
- Discuss the characters – were they believable and could you relate to them?
- How important was the setting to the story?
- Are the themes timeless?
- Personal reactions – what did you like or not like about the book?

There is a free toolkit with lots of ideas to help you run a Quick Reads reading group at **www.quickreads.org.uk**

Share your experiences of your group on Twitter 🐦 @Quick_Reads

For more ideas, offers and groups to join visit Reading Groups for Everyone at **www.readingagency.org.uk/readinggroups**

Other resources

Enjoy this book?

Find out about all the others at **www.quickreads.org.uk**

For Quick Reads audio clips as well as videos
and ideas to help you enjoy reading visit the
BBC's Skillswise website **www.bbc.co.uk/quickreads**

Join the Reading Agency's Six Book Challenge at
www.readingagency.org.uk/sixbookchallenge

THE
READING
AGENCY

Find more books for new readers at
www.newisland.ie
www.barringtonstoke.co.uk

Barrington Stoke
cracking reading

Free courses to develop your skills are available in your
local area. To find out more phone 0800 100 900.

National
Careers
Service
Helping you take
the next step

For more information on developing your skills
in Scotland visit **www.thebigplus.com**

the big plus

Want to read more? Join your local library. You can borrow
books for free and take part in inspiring reading activities.

Lynda La Plante

BACKLASH

Two unsolved murders. Three confessions. One suspect.

**But is the man in DCI Anna Travis's custody
a serial killer ... or just a compulsive liar?**

It is late at night on a notorious council estate in
east London when the police pull over a van.
Inside, they discover the body of a young woman.

The driver confesses, not just to one murder – but to three.

Five years earlier, a 13-year-old girl disappeared in
broad daylight on a busy London street. The unsolved
case has haunted DCS James Langton ever since.
But when the case is reopened, it falls to Anna
to investigate and bring the killer to trial.

Meanwhile, the murder team is hard at work verifying
the details of the van driver's confessions and desperately
trying to uncover the identities of his other victims.

And then he changes his story ...

Paperback ISBN 978-1-84983-336-3
Ebook ISBN 978-0-85720-185-0

Lynda La Plante
THE LEGACY

For three people, 'The Legacy' was a curse ...

Hugh, a hard-drinking lion of the Welsh valleys.
His daughter Evelyne – who lost her heart to a
travelling gypsy. And handsome prizefighter
Freedom – saved from the gallows to do battle
for the heavyweight championship of the world.

From the poverty of the Welsh pit valleys to the glories
of the prize ring, from the dangers of Prohibition America
to the terrors of Britain at war, Lynda La Plante delves
into the lives of a remarkable family and its fortunes,
and the curse that forged their names.

'A torrid tale of love, intrigue and passion' – *Daily Express*

Paperback ISBN 978-1-47110-024-6
Ebook ISBN 978-1-47110-026-0

Lynda La Plante
THE TALISMAN

What will the future hold for a family cursed by its past?

As Gypsy tradition dictates, Freedom Stubbs should
have been buried with the gold necklace that he earned
as a Heavyweight Boxing Champion. Instead, his wife
Evelyne kept it, hoping to sell it for a hefty profit if ever
the family were to fall on hard times. As a result, the
family is afflicted by a terrible curse.

Freedom's sons, Edward and Alex, suffer the consequences
of their family's past mistake, as a series of horrifying
events fuels the brothers' lust for justice. Struggling to
survive, will they be able to keep their loved ones safe?

From the miseries of war years to the glamorous present,
in London, America and South Africa, Lynda La Plante
continues the bestselling saga that began with *The Legacy*.
The passionate story of a family's lives and fortunes,
and the curse that forged their names ...

Paperback ISBN 978-1-47113-081-6
Ebook ISBN 978-1-47113-082-3

Lynda La Plante
PRIME SUSPECT

When a prostitute is found murdered in her bedsit, the Metropolitan police set to work finding the perpetrator of this brutal attack. DNA samples lead them straight to George Marlow, a man previously convicted of attempted rape. Everything appears to add up and the police think they've found their man, but things aren't quite what they seem ...

Detective Chief Inspector Jane Tennison came through the ranks the hard way, opposed and resented at every step by her male colleagues. So when DCI Shefford falls ill, the opportunity for Tennison to get herself noticed finally arrives. But the boys are not happy and every one of her colleagues is willing her to trip up.

Desperate to remove all doubt around her suspect, Tennison struggles to make the charges stick. And then a second body turns up. With the team against her, and a dangerous criminal still on the loose, DCI Jane Tennison must fight to prove herself, now or never.

Paperback ISBN 978-1-47110-021-5
Ebook ISBN 978-1-47110-023-9

Lynda La Plante

PRIME SUSPECT 2:
A FACE IN THE CROWD

The coroner's report identifies the body as young,
black, female and anonymous. Yet one thing is clear to
Detective Chief Inspector Jane Tennison about the latest
victim discovered in one of London's poorest districts –
that news of her murder will tear apart a city already
cracking with racial tensions, hurling Scotland Yard
and Tennison herself into a maelstrom of
shocking accusations and sudden violence.

As London's ruthless killer remains at large, Tennison
is struggling to overcome her station house's brutal
chauvinism and insidious politicking. And as the
department's deeply rooted racism overshadows every
facet of her new investigation, the trail of her prime suspect
grows colder. Worse, when details of the beleaguered
detective's stormy personal life explode across the
headlines of London's sleaziest tabloids, Tennison's
already frenzied determination to bring the killer to
justice will be catapulted into obsession – one that
could send her spiralling over the edge.

Paperback ISBN 978-1-47111-492-2
Ebook ISBN 978-1-47111-493-9

Lynda La Plante

PRIME SUSPECT 3:
SILENT VICTIMS

Chief Detective Inspector Jane Tennison has moved up
the ranks, fighting every step of the way to break through
the station house's glass ceiling. Now, on her first day
as the head of the Vice Squad, a case comes in that
threatens to destroy everything she has worked for.

As Vera Reynolds, drag queen and night club star, swayed
onstage singing 'Falling in Love Again', a sixteen-year-old
rent boy lay in the older man's apartment, engulfed
in flames. When Tennison's investigation reveals an
influential public figure as her prime suspect, a man
with connections to politicians, judges and Scotland Yard,
she's given a very clear message about the direction some
very important people would like her investigation to take.

Suddenly, in a case defined by murky details, one fact
becomes indisputably clear – that for Tennison,
going after the truth will mean risking her
happiness, her career and even her life.

Paperback ISBN 978-1-47111-494-6
Ebook ISBN 978-1-47111-495-3

Lynda La Plante

SHE'S OUT

They locked her up in Holloway for murder ... but now that she's out, she has unfinished business to attend to.

After serving a lengthy sentence for shooting her husband at point blank range, Dolly Rawlins is set free from prison, with only one thing on her mind – the six million in diamonds she stashed prior to her imprisonment.

Waiting for Dolly is a group of women who all served time with her. They know about the diamonds and they want a cut. Also waiting is a detective sergeant in the Metropolitan Police. He holds her personally responsible for the death of his sister in the diamond raid ten years earlier. And now he wants her back inside.

Dolly Rawlins has other plans: to realise the dream that kept her going for years in prison. But against such determined opposition, the fantasy soon turns into a very different, tragic and violent reality ...

Paperback ISBN 978-1-47110-027-7
Ebook ISBN 978-1-47110-029-1